WELCOME TO
PASSPORT TO READING
A beginning reader's ticket to a brand-new world!

Every book in this program is designed to build read-along and read-alone skills, level by level, through engaging and enriching stories. As the reader turns each page, he or she will become more confident with new vocabulary, sight words, and comprehension.

These PASSPORT TO READING levels will help you choose the perfect book for every reader.

READING TOGETHER
Read short words in simple sentence structures together to begin a reader's journey.

READING OUT LOUD
Encourage developing readers to sound out words in more complex stories with simple vocabulary.

READING INDEPENDENTLY
Newly independent readers gain confidence reading more complex sentences with higher word counts.

READY TO READ MORE
Readers prepare for chapter books with fewer illustrations and longer paragraphs.

This book features sight words from the educator-supported Dolch Sight Words List. This encourages the reader to recognize commonly used vocabulary words, increasing reading speed and fluency.

Enjoy the journey!

ABDOPUBLISHING.COM

Reinforced library bound edition published in 2018 by Spotlight, a division of ABDO, PO Box 398166, Minneapolis, Minnesota 55439. Spotlight produces high-quality reinforced library bound editions for schools and libraries. Published by agreement with Little, Brown and Company.

Printed in the United States of America, North Mankato, Minnesota.
092017
012018

Licensed By:

HASBRO and its logo, MY LITTLE PONY and all related characters are trademarks of Hasbro and are used with permission. © 2017 Hasbro. All Rights Reserved.

Little, Brown and Company

Hachette Book Group, 1290 Avenue of the Americas, New York, NY 10104

Little, Brown and Company is a division of Hachette Book Group, Inc.
The Little, Brown name and logo are trademarks of Hachette Book Group, Inc.

PUBLISHER'S CATALOGING IN PUBLICATION DATA

Names: Belle, Magnolia, author. | Hasbro Studios, illustrator.
Title: We are family / writer, Magnolia Belle ; art, Hasbro Studios.
Description: Reinforced library edition. | Minneapolis, Minnesota : Spotlight, 2018. |
    Series: My little pony leveled readers
Summary: Get to know all of your favorite ponies and their different families!
Identifiers: LCCN 2017943448 | ISBN 9781532140983
Subjects: LCSH: Leveled reader--Juvenile fiction. | Ponies--Juvenile fiction. | Family--
    Juvenile fiction.
Classification: DDC [E]--dc23
LC record available at https://lccn.loc.gov/2017943448

Spotlight

A Division of ABDO
abdopublishing.com

My Little Pony

We Are Family

written by **Magnolia Belle**

L B

LITTLE, BROWN AND COMPANY
New York Boston

ABDO
Spotlight

Attention, My Little Pony fans!
Look for these words when you read this book.
Can you spot them all?

Castle of Friendship

magic

bakery

sports teams

In Ponyville, family is as
important as friendship!

Twilight Sparkle is a
part of many families.

Twilight lives in the Castle of Friendship with Spike.

He is her best friend!

She also lives with her pet,
Owlowiscious.

Twilight loves Spike and Owlowiscious.
They are a family!

Twilight loves her parents, too.
She is great at magic because
her parents are Unicorns, too!

Twilight has a brother.
Shining Armor is married
to Princess Cadance.

They have a baby named Flurry Heart.
Twilight is Flurry Heart's aunt!

Flurry Heart is not the only baby
in Equestria.

Mr. and Mrs. Cake's twins are named
Pound Cake and Pumpkin Cake.

Fluttershy also has a brother.

His name is Zephyr Breeze.

Twilight and Fluttershy do not have
sisters, but Pinkie Pie has three!
They work with their parents.

Rarity also has a little sister.

She is very helpful.

Her name is Sweetie Belle.

Applejack has a brother and sister.
Big McIntosh and Apple Bloom
live with Granny Smith.
She takes good care of them.

Rainbow Dash does not have
a sister or brother.
She is an only child.
She looks out for Scootaloo
like a big sister.

Sometimes brothers and sisters fight
and hurt one another's feelings.
And sometimes they are the
best of friends.

Princess Celestia and Princess Luna
were mad at each other.
Now they are friends again.

Sometimes families live together
or get together for parties...

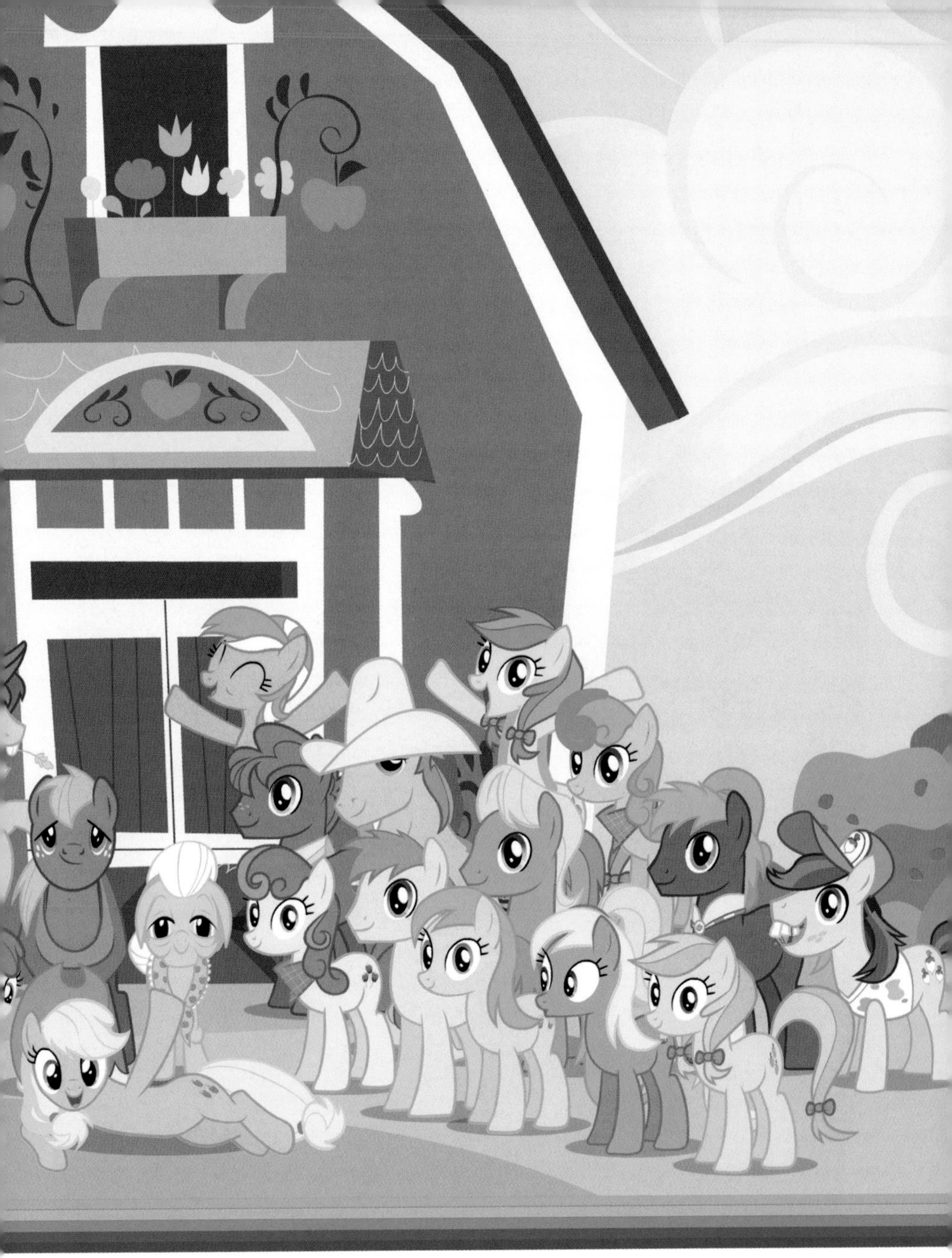

...like the Apple family.

And sometimes the ponies and friends who live together become a family, like Twilight and Spike.

Fluttershy has lots of pets.

She treats them like family.

They love Fluttershy very much.

Opalescence is Rarity's cat.

She is part of her family.

Pinkie lives with the Cake family.

She works with them in their bakery.

They help one another like family.

Sports teams are another
kind of family.
The Wonderbolts train
together every day.

Best friends are also like a family.

The Cutie Mark Crusaders are

like sisters.

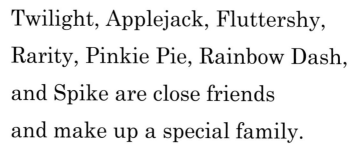

Twilight, Applejack, Fluttershy, Rarity, Pinkie Pie, Rainbow Dash, and Spike are close friends and make up a special family.

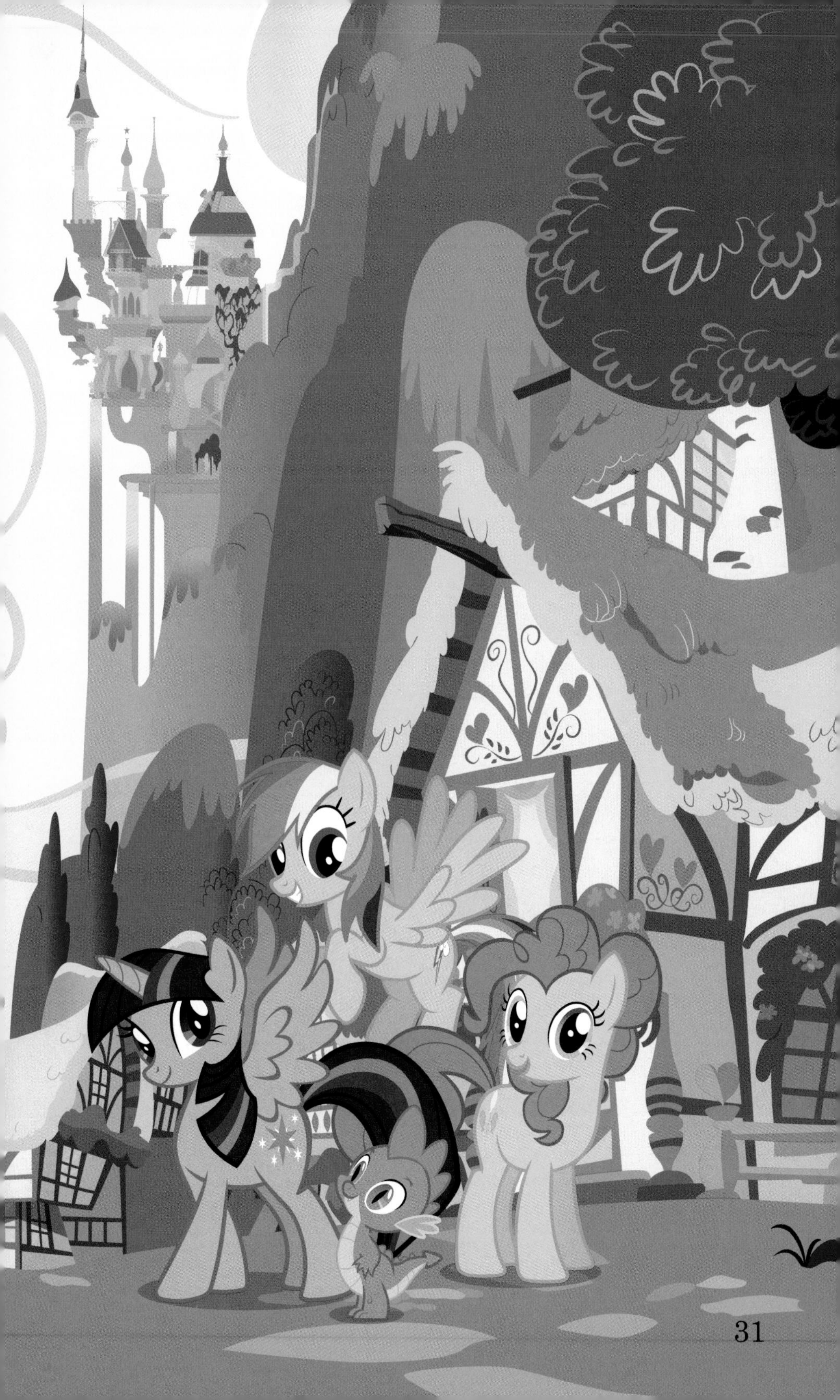

No matter where a pony lives,
they are with their family
when they feel love.